HER ROYAL MAJESTY, THE SUPERHERO BRIDE OF FRANKENSTEIN

Written and Illustrated
by
Melinda Taliancich Falgoust

Printed in the United States of America

First Printing, 2015

Wagging Tales Press

P.O. Box 113294

Metairie, LA 70011-3294

www.waggingtalespress.com

It was the single, worst moment of Lizzie's eight years – a tragic occurrence of Lizzie's worst fear.

It wasn't a skeleton, ghost, wolf, or mummy.

It was something quite common, but something quite funny.

An embarrassing moment stuck fast to her shoe,

trailing out through the door and down the hall, too.

It rolled past the pumpkins
with looks of surprise...

...past Janitor Wilkins,

who widened his eyes...

...past the Halloween banner hung over the lockers...

...and into the bathroom...

TOILET PAPER!

What a shocker.

All the kids in the class and the boy with red hair

laughed and pointed to Lizzie. Each one of them stared.

Every girl giggled hard until tears filled her eyes.

Boys howled till it sounded like chimps were inside.

Lizzie's face turned as red
as a fire truck's paint.
Her freckles connected.
She started to faint.
But, just as she tried
to crawl under her seat,
the teacher announced
their Halloween treat!

"Good morning, class!"
Teacher greeted the room.
"We're having a contest,
the winner of whom,
will earn the position,
but just for a day,
of Principal." Everyone
shouted hooray.

The teacher continued.
"The best costume wins!"
And mean Sophie Tucker
just started to grin.
"Lizzie's already got
a costume just right.
A roll of T.P.!"
She sneered out of spite.

Lizzie wished that the ground
would swallow her whole.
They were all poking fun
just because of a roll!
When all of a sudden,
the most perfect plan
popped into her head.
She just waved her hand.

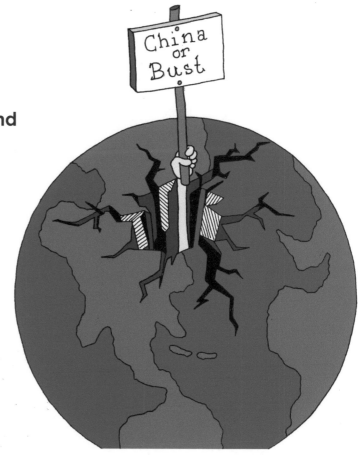

"What are you doing?" Sophie asked nosily.

"I'm Queen Lizzy, of course. Here's my train. Can't you see?"

She was waving quite royally all the way to her seat,

while the paper trailed regally there at her feet.

"So very clever!" the teacher then said.

But, the laughter still rippled. Liz scratched her head.

She gathered the paper, stuffed some into her shirt.

In a hero-like voice, she started to blurt.

"Dum dee dee dah!" Then, just like a cape,

the paper flew out like a long flowing drape.

"I can add double-digits in one single try!

Strong enough to shoot chocolate milk from my eye!"

The giggles continued,
but started to change.
Lizzie's fun was contagious.
It was almost a game.

"Give us another!
One scary and fun."
Lizzie thought for a moment
and came up with one.

She tousled her hair and teased up the height.

Then she weaved in the paper, a bold strip of white.

"I'm Frankenstein's Bride." She moaned kind of spooky,

then walked with straight legs. It looked kind of kooky.

"Such clever ideas," the teacher proposed.

But, mean Sophie Tucker just stuck up her nose.

"My costume's better, the greatest around.

I'll be the best, the winner hands down!"

"Why, Sophie!" fussed Teacher. "That's terribly rude.

You'll never win anything with THAT attitude."

Sophie said sorry, but Lizzie could tell

her fingers were crossed (a few toes as well).

The bell clamored loudly to signal for lunch.

They stumbled together, a Halloween bunch.

Dracula's cape fluttered over the Zombie,

who stepped on the tail of the Werewolf named Tommy.

"Off with the costumes!" the teacher declared.

"Hang every one up. After lunch, they'll be there."

The children obeyed. Even Drac left his teeth.

Each one except Sophie. (That *horrible* sneak!)

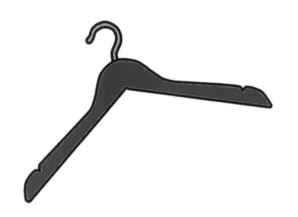

When the children returned
They were shocked and alarmed.
The costumes were missing!
Each one of them...GONE!

"Start up a search!" the teacher proclaimed.
"They've certainly got to be here!"
And the children did search,
up high and down low, quite far
and also quite near.

They looked in the bowl
that held the class fish.
They looked,
but nothing was there.

They looked in the gym.
They searched the whole band.

They looked in the lunch
lady's hair.

The minutes ticked by.

The party was close.

Not one costume

could even be found.

Lizzie heard a small giggle

and thought it was strange, so,

wisely, she followed the sound.

Sophie looked smug,
her arms folded tight.
Lizzie suspected foul play...

...when a brilliant idea
came all at once.
Super Lizzie could save the day!

With just minutes left
before the big bash,
Lizzie scooped up her pile of tissue.
She tore it in pieces,
some big and some small,
to solve the class
lost costume issue.

She wrapped Ben up tight,
like an old Pharaoh mummy,
and Jill, she turned into a ghost.
Tommy was changed
to a masked, caped avenger
(the costume that Lizzie liked
most).

Lizzie whirled and she twirled. She made prim ballerinas.

She cut and she snipped and she tied.

And when she was finished, each kid was disguised.

She sighed and she looked on with pride.

Sophie just sneered. She curled up her lip.

"There's still no way you can win.

You don't have a costume 'cause everyone else

is wearing your paper inventions."

Lizzie looked down. Sophie was right.

There was not even one extra inch.

She'd helped all her friends make their costumes, but now

she found herself in a pinch.

The bell jangled loudly. The children lined up.

It was finally time for the party.

Lizzie wasn't too sad. She had done the right thing.

Sophie wasn't that much of a smarty.

The party was fun. There were lots of great games—

Pin-the-Nose-on-the-Pumpkin and then

Bobbing-for-Apples and then it was time

to find out exactly who'd win.

Third place went to Tommy.
He might have scored second,
but he pinned his nose
on the teacher.

Ben, the Mummy, took second
for looking just like
the late-night T.V.
creature feature.

First place went to Addy and Abby Adair—

twin tutus flying high overhead.

The children all clapped. They whooped and they cheered.

Teacher signaled for quiet instead.

"The costumes were grand. We loved every one,

but the best, the top of the line,

goes to the girl who made every one—

Her Royal Majesty, the Superhero

Bride of Frankenstein."

CPSIA information can be obtained
at www.ICGtesting.com
Printed in the USA
LVHW072313120319
610459LV00006B/32/P